HIDDEN PAGES
The Story of **Sapali**

SUSI MOSIS
SIMBA OGBEBOR MOSIS

Copyright © by Serendipitist Inc. B.V. 2023

All rights reserved. No part of this publication may be reproduced, distributed, or transmitted in any form or by any means, including photocopying, recording, or other electronic or mechanical methods, without the prior written permission of the publisher, except in the case of brief quotations embodied in critical reviews and certain other noncommercial uses permitted by copyright law.

Made possible by Sisa Events Foundation

Authors: Susi Mosis & Simba Ogbebor Mosis
Co-author & Art Director: Sentini Grunberg
Executive Producer: Georgio Mosis
Illustrator: Francis Greenslade
Editor: Vera Peters

Publishing by Jungo Books
www.jungo.app

Appreciation Of Your Own Traditional Heritage

Table of Contents

Foreword vii

Introduction 11

CHAPTER 1
An Uncertain Journey 15

CHAPTER 2
The New Land 31

CHAPTER 3
An Ingenious Plan 43

CHAPTER 4
Escape To Where? 59

CHAPTER 5
Boobiabla 71

Acknowledgement 79

Glossary 81

Foreword

For generations, the stories about the freedom fights of the Maroons were passed on orally and within the community. Unfortunately, this explains why these stories today are still unknown to a large part of the Surinamese community and others.

In The Story of Sapali, Susi and Simba Mosis take the reader back to the cruel period of slavery in eighteenth-century Surinam. The main character in the book is Sapali, a young woman with almost superhuman strength and intelligence. Sapali's strategic insight has not only led to her freedom, but she also helped many others achieve the same.

With this book, Susi and Simba emphatically place themselves in the category of writers who take a different approach and describe the enslaved people in a way that reflects their deepest strength. In addition, they make a promising start by unveiling the hidden history of the Maroon community.

We are grateful for Susi and Simba and everyone who inspired and supported them during the writing process. We especially thank the ancestors who have passed on this knowledge to them.

Lillian Callender

The fundamental essence of one's life is knowing where one came from, where one is going, what one is doing, and why one is doing it. Our story of slavery, this is true for all blacks around the world, especially the Maroon populations in Surinam, needs to be told. The identity of the enslaved was the first to be shattered by the significant treatment of transatlantic slavery as self-knowledge is essential for our individual growth. A system that is genuinely the biggest human rights violation ever, cannot be forgotten. Slaves did not have the same rights as free people and were not considered as human beings. Racism and other forms of discrimination we are experiencing today everywhere in the world are effectively the consequences of slavery.

We all know there is already a sizable body of historical writings about slavery, but this book is unique. Hidden Pages, The Story of Sapali, is so much more than simply another historical book because of its hidden "chapters". It is a book that asserts black people's authority. It pierces down to the core of a troubling past that is still felt today. Sapali's courageous life has been brilliantly brought to life in a lovely, intriguing, heart-warming, and humorous manner by Susi and Simba Mosis. The descendants of slaves should be proud of their history, knowing what they have achieved since the foundation of the first black republic in Haiti in 1804 after a glorious defeat inflicted on the Napoleon army, the first world military power back then. In order to continue on the route already walked by our ancestors with pride, let's not forget where we came from.

As my mother would say: Gado-afisie, Gado-abaka! (God before and behind us).

I guarantee that all of you, who read this book, will get a compass from which to draw power to mend a shattered history. Above all, let's keep recording our history for the sake of present and future generations and for the glory of our ancestors. The power of knowledge. The ability that ought to allow us to look ahead. This book accurately portrays who we are: courageous people.

Titinbo Erna Aviankoi

Introduction

As we sat in our living room, surrounded by our younger cousins and kids, Susi and I couldn't help but feel proud as they admired the wooden sculptures that we had brought from our village in Surinam. Our kids and cousins were curious and wanted to know more about our heritage, which led to a fascinating conversation about the African diaspora and the impact of the slave trade on our people.

As twins, we had always been taught about the remarkable bravery and intelligence of a woman named Sapali through oral tradition. Sapali played a vital role in helping our ancestors escape from slavery and establish their own village. We had grown up listening to stories of her heroism, and we knew that she was celebrated in songs by different tribes, making her a significant figure in our culture.

These stories have been passed down from generation to generation for over 500 years through oral tradition as a way to preserve our cultural identity. We felt a deep connection to these stories and knew that it was our generation's responsibility to turn these oral histories into written pages, so they would not be forgotten.

The Story of Sapali is a fictional retelling of this historical event based on the oral tradition that has been passed down to us. We hope that this story will inspire future generations to embrace their heritage and celebrate the strength and resilience of our people. Through this book, we honor the memory of our ancestors who fought for their freedom and hope to inspire others to learn more about the rich history of African American culture.

With love and respect,

Susi and Simba

Photo by Erik Smits Photography

CHAPTER 1

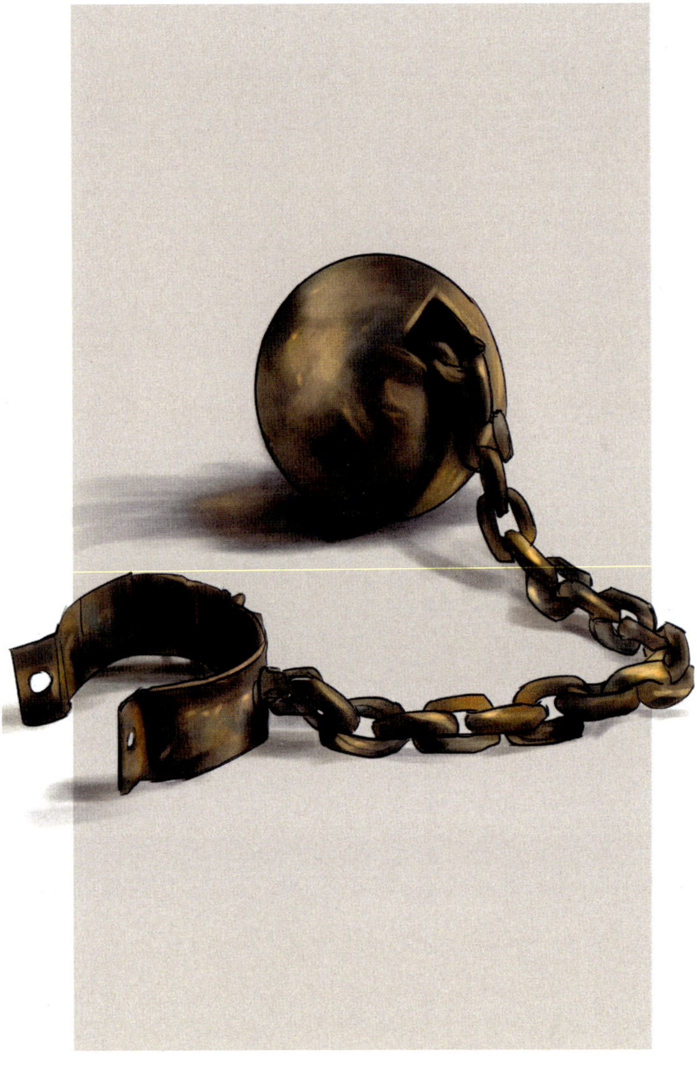

An Uncertain Journey

Sapali was staring into the distance. Suddenly something on the water arrived. It was as big as the mountains. Her people had been living in the mountains, and she loved how majestic it looked. But how can a mountain be on the water? She looked more closely as the enormous object approached the shore. She saw there were people on it. The people were looking strange… they had the same color as the sand of the beach she was standing on. They were pale, and some of their faces were red like the insides of a watermelon.

As the object approached, Sapali saw it was a boat, but way bigger than she was used to seeing in the streams near her village. She had never seen a strange-looking and huge one like this. It almost looked like a monster with all the long poles sticking out and many big white pieces of cloth that were attached to them. She saw the wind was blowing, and the cloth was bulging. She quickly figured it out: "The big cloth is probably used to help the big boat move forward."

The waves were strong that day. She felt scared and looked down at her hands… The chains were heavy, painful and way too tight. She had heard from the women next to her that the *sand-faced* people had said that they would soon be removed. It was temporary to get into that big mountain on the water. Her body felt heavy and tired.. Her *kente* dress was still looking neat, even though they had been traveling for days to get to the beach. It was the only colorful happy item she could take from her village. All her belongings were gone. She felt the beads under her dress as they were pressing on her waist. It was a very hot day. The sun shone brightly on her coco skin, and she looked at the sweat drops falling down her arms and how they rolled into the chains around her wrist. Her skin was shimmering and looked like a black diamond. Her body was slim, and her physique was athletic and strong. Her hair was big and stood up towards the sun.

She looked behind her. In the other row, there was a group of men that were chained together. One of them was staring at her with a strong gaze. Their eyes locked in... Sapali felt shy and looked away. She felt a strange feeling in her belly. She looked back to see if he was still staring at her but saw that he was looking down. At his feet, there were double the amount of shackles that she had. A feeling of anger overtook her: "Breathe, Sapali, breathe," she said to herself to calm down.

She remembered her time in her village, where she had felt that same feeling in her belly when looking at a young man. Where would her mother and brother be? Before they were captured, her dad had disappeared. No one knew what had happened to all the elders of her village. Her dad had been a part of the village council. Were they taken away to another place, ...or worse? Sapali had heard stories of people disappearing behind the horizon of the sea, never to be returned. It had been happening for a while, and they thought it had something to do with a punishment from the ancestors.

"All aboard!" the man with the big hat and blue cloth shouted. His clothes were so tight on his body. And he was completely covered from head to toe. His arms and legs were fully covered, and he had a hat on, which threw a shadow over his pale face. Sapali didn't understand what the man was saying. *"It is a strange language these people are speaking,"* she thought to herself.

The man noticed that Sapali was looking at him. He hastily approached her and grabbed her arm. She wanted to protest and retreat her arm. But from the corner of her eyes, she saw that the man she had locked eyes with earlier was staring at her again and was nodding his head silently from left to right. "No…, he is saying no…" Sapali immediately forced herself to calm down again while the man unshackled her from the long chain of women she was attached to. "Where will he take me? What is happening?" She was furious and scared. The *sand-faced* man's grip was firm. "How dare he grab my arm so violently!" As they were walking, she couldn't stop thinking of finding a way out to escape this madness. To be back under the big trees and see the green leaves providing shade and coolness. "In the mountains, my *kente* dress never stuck to my body and legs like this… It's so hot here!"

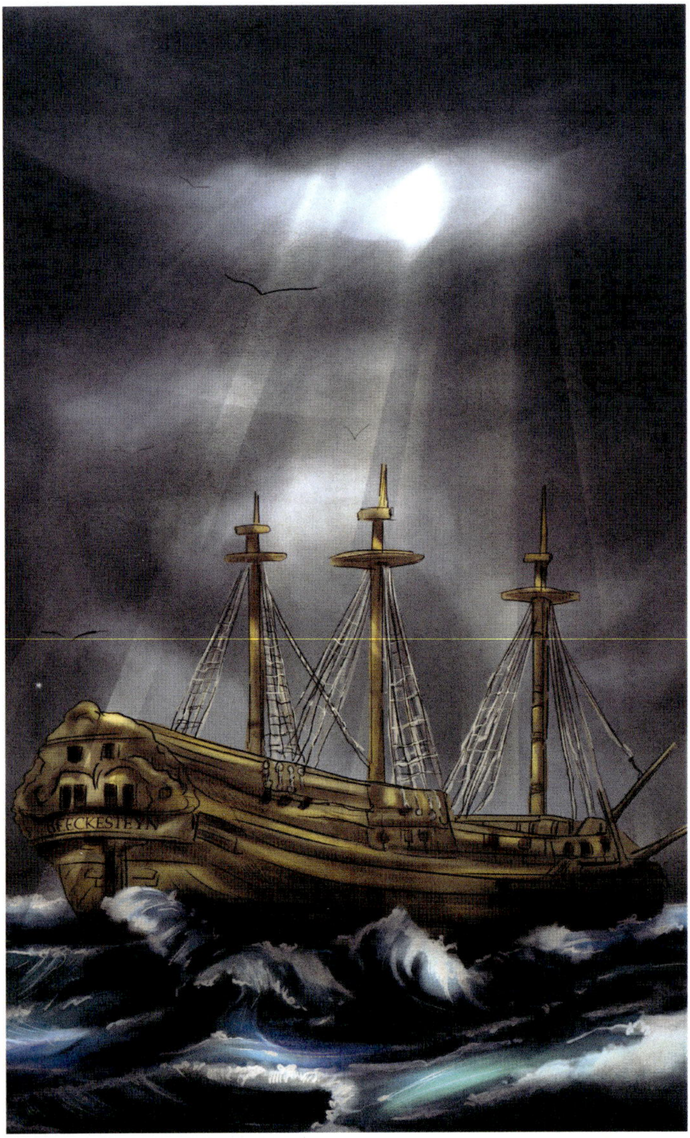
ECKESTEYN

The man walked with her through a mass of people; it was so crowded that the people looked like the ants she used to chase in the village as a little girl. Even though they were well hidden, she always found ants' nests and saw how they were crawling over each other. The ants' nests were always chaotic yet organized. That's exactly how this place was. It was a terrible place; people were locking eyes with her as she passed the rows of men and women who were all chained. Some were sitting ,some were standing, and some were praying to their ancestors while looking up at the sky. Others were crying while they looked at the ocean, imagining themselves having an imminent death.

Sapali had never seen the ocean before. She had only heard about it. Her people were from the mountains, a proud tribe with high spiritual values. Sapali knew the rivers that were around the mountains where she lived at the back of her hands. She had heard about the ocean from her older cousins, who had been married off to another tribe. They visited the village once when they had children, and their husbands still had some business with our tribe. Sapali suspected that her people being captured had something to do with the argument that took place between her cousin's husbands and the village council, which her father was a part of. Was it a setup? The road to her village was hard to find. Only people close to her tribe knew about it, as it was set up in a way that looked like you could not reach there. It was her safe haven… Suddenly she feels that her cheeks are wet, and she realizes she is crying. For the first time, after all these horrible events, she is crying. Both from anger, frustration, sadness, confusion… Sapali had always dreamt of seeing the ocean but never thought it would happen under these terrible circumstances.

Ayye!! Ayye!! A man on the top of the big boat was screaming. Suddenly, Sapali was rudely awakened from her thoughts. She saw that she was brought to the front of the crowd, and the man let her be attached to a new group of women.

"Shall my mom and brother also be here? What will these people do? Will they bring us into the water to drown? Suddenly, her curiosity turned into sadness."

The women around her were crying silently, many looking back with tears on their cheeks. She had never seen so many women cry at the same time. It was like one big herd of despair. I don't know if I will ever see my mother or my brother again... The women started to hum... As they all entered the slave ship, all mothers, daughters, nieces, aunts, grandmothers, and granddaughters started to hum as one. All generations, from all walks of life... Stuck in one situation with one wish. To be free.

The boat was filled with so many people. Sapali felt like she was suffocating because there were so many people close to each other. The smell of sweat and fear was everywhere. The loud humming that had been taking place while entering the ship had been replaced by silence. Here and there, you heard people crying. It was like the whole ship got strangely quiet. It suddenly got real that they were going to leave behind the land that they had known since birth, where their ancestors had been living as long as they could remember.

A woman with big scars on her face was chained to the left of Sapali and whispered to her, "they will kill us all; they will throw us in the water. That's what they do." Sapali felt a sense of panic inside of her. Then she turned to the right, where another woman was looking at her. She was a bit younger than the woman on her left. Her eyes were big and filled with fear, like the eyes of a goat right before they are slaughtered. The girl was about her age. Not yet a woman, but also not a girl anymore. She had definitely already been through the rituals to transform from girl to woman —just like Sapali had gone through back in the village. Sapali was considered a young woman but she still felt like a girl as she felt she hadn't learned enough yet. She had been ripped away from her aunts, her mother, and her grandmother and had no idea where they were. "How will they teach me to be an honorable woman? How will I learn the ways of my tribe?" Thinking of her family was too much to bear. She swallowed to prevent the tears from rolling down her eyes again. *"To be a woman means that I must be strong even in the face of adversity,"* she said to herself. That is something that she used to always hear from her mom.

After a short while, the girl on the left broke her silence and started to speak; her eyes looked less big. She said her name was Ama. Ama was named after the day that she was born; that is what many tribes do. The boat was filled with different tribes. Some of them spoke languages Sapali had never heard. Luckily, the woman and the girl next to her spoke the same language as her. Ama continued and said to Sapali: "Somebody told me once that there is a distant land where they take our people to work and be slaves. I went to the elders in my village, but they were saying that it was all a lie. That it wasn't true and that people could say anything to scare us. I think they wanted to protect the people in the village to not be scared." She turned her head to Sapali and looks at her with a sense of sadness, and says: "Wouldn't it have been better if the fighters in our villages had been prepared? Why would they hide this from us?"

Sapali and Ama were abruptly disturbed by their short conversation as the big ship started moving. She noticed a hole in the wooden bench under her and peeked through it. She saw that a group of men who were captured just like her were rowing the big ship. So it wasn't only the wind and the bulging cloth that made this monstrosity move. It was the people who made this enormous thing move… our people.

The big ship started moving. As they pulled away from the shore, Sapali couldn't help but let out a big scream of despair. She was sobbing, her body shaking uncontrollably as if she had caught a fever. "Why, ancestors, why does this happen to me? To us? What have we done to be ripped away from our land like this? What do these people want?" The ship entered deep waters and began to rock more heavily from side to side. Sapali began to feel sick. She hadn't eaten much on the long journey from the mountains to the beach and missed eating the fufu she used to prepare in her village. Her stomach felt weird; she needed to throw up, and before she knew it, the content of her stomach was on the wooden floor of the ship. She looked up and felt ashamed. *"Will I feel sick this whole journey?"* she thought to herself.

"Where would we end up? Was it true what the woman on her right had said, that they would just throw them overboard? But why would these *sand-faced* people go to such great lengths to capture them if all they would do is just kill everyone?" It didn't make sense to her.

Sapali woke up in a scare. Apparently, she had fallen asleep, but a rhythmic sound woke her up. It was like someone was playing a drum. She looked to the far left side of the ship and saw a familiar silhouette . It was that man, the one she had seen in the row of people behind her. Her protector. They got separated but somehow ended up close enough to each other to exchange looks. Sapali took her time to take a good look at him. He had strong arms and a big chest. As soon as he felt her eyes piercing, he looked up and started staring at her. His gaze was a bit lighter now. It was still intense, but there was a sense of kindness in his eyes. Even a light smile. She looked at his lips, they were full, and he kept them slightly separated from each other. Something about him was different than all the other young men who had shown interest in her. He had something special. Even while he was in chains, he still protected her. Because who knows what the *sand-faced* man in the dark blue cloth would have done to her if she had protested. She thought to herself: *"From now I will have to keep my cool and divert from acting up and observe the situation before I make a move. I have to."*

In the mornings, the women were put to work to peel maize and remove rice grains from the grass stalks to prepare food for the crew and other captives on the ship. These crops were brought onto the ship from their African homeland. There were so many bags filled with beans, corn, yams, rice, and palm oil, yet her people didn't get much to eat. They were fed one meal a day with water, if at all. When food was scarce, the *sand-faced* people would get priority over them. They called the *sand-faced* people many names; some were human traders, and those were the ones that captured her and her people. The shippers were the ones who controlled the journey with their big boats.

Even though she was part of the people who prepared the food, she ate barely enough to survive. "Ama told me that we are going to a distant land. If this is true, we can escape when we arrive," she thought to herself. Sapali remembered the jollof rice dishes they were eating back in her village. Those were good times. She did not even realize how great her life had been until now. Sapali looked around in fear. The women minded their business, and everyone was focused on working as fast as possible as they did not want to run the risk of punishment. When no one was watching, Sapali hastily hid a couple of rice grains in her thick hair.

While the women were preparing the food, they were usually singing. Some were songs that Sapali didn't know as they were sung in different languages and were from tribes other than hers. Sapali was from the *Ashanti* tribe, a tribe that was very highly regarded in her region. They were known for gold and brass craftsmanship, wood carving, furniture, and brightly colored woven cloth called *kente*. There were people from the Igbo tribe known for their enterprising, independent, and adventurous nature. The Fanti are known for their distinct traditional clothing and food. And then you had the Mandingos.

They were really big and tall and known for their drumming and unique musical instruments. Some tunes were familiar to her, and then she sang out loud. When they were allowed to sing, it almost felt like she was back in the village. The festivities used to be amazing, and singing, they used to dance with the guidance of the talking drum. Drumming was a powerful source of communication and was used for so many purposes. Different rhythms and patterns of drumming were crafted to communicate messages, like a warning of danger, inviting people to a ceremony, or bringing tribes together to celebrate. Even a village's ancestral history might be shared through the beat of a drum. In some instances, song and dance would accompany the drum rhythm, creating an even more spiritual atmosphere. Sapali always danced with so much fire and passion. Everyone in the village knew she was a great dancer. And she loved to show off. Sadly on the boat, there was not much room for dancing.

In the distance, the men were using their shackles and their hands on the wooden walls of the boat to make a drumming sound. It transmitted information and emotions to all the Africans on the ship. They were creating this soundscape where the drums echoed through the air, connecting people of the various tribes who were stuck in the same predicament. The rhythmic drumming sounds helped the captives to remain strong and endure each uncertain day. At daybreak, Sapali walked over to serve the men in the slave's cabins. Even though the circumstances were terrible, Sapali tried to serve food that they had just prepared with pride. She held her head up as she walked over to the men in chains. Most of them had big and strong physiques, just like the *Apintieman*. That's what Sapali had decided to call the man, who had practically been her savior before entering the ship and had been staring at her many times from a distance. Every time she walked past him or served him food, he never said a word. This time it was different. She wanted to walk to the next person, but the *Apintieman* stopped her and grabbed her hand softly, and said: "Listen carefully to the sounds of the rhythm I make and know that what I'm saying comes from my heart." Sapali smiled nervously, nodded, and walked off. While serving the others, she couldn't stop hiding the little smile on her face. No one really noticed her changed mood; everyone was busy with their sorrows. For Sapali, it was a special day; it was the first time in a long while that she genuinely smiled. Her heart felt full.

Every day at dawn, when she prepared the food with the women, she heard him play. She imagined his handsome face and his broad chest. *"He probably is from the Mandingo tribe,"* Sapali thought to herself. They are known for being excellent at drumming patterns. He played various types of rhythms on the different wooden parts of the ship and often drummed on his chest. Slowly but surely, she began to understand what he was saying with his drumming patterns. His drumming sounds were a code language in which he even could say complex things. Mostly, the patterns were uplifting for the people on the ship to not give up hope. Sometimes he went over to complex rhythms. Sapali knew that the people who used to play these drum sounds were specially chosen in the village. Not just anyone can put complex meanings encoded in the drum patterns like this. It meant he had to have been trained since he was a small boy to communicate in a way that spoke to the audience. Sapali had learned to recognize when he was communicating with the whole ship and when he specifically was talking to her with his drumming sounds. She remembers back in the village when the talking drum was so special, and her brother was one of those who was learning how to play it. She then sneaked along to watch how they were teaching him to play, and therefore she knew some of the code languages that were embedded in the various rhythms. Now she was determined to learn to understand even the most complicated codes embedded in the drum. Sapali had always had a strong musical memory, and she started to recognize the melodies and coded messages her admirer was communicating to her with his drumming as each day passed.

CHAPTER 2

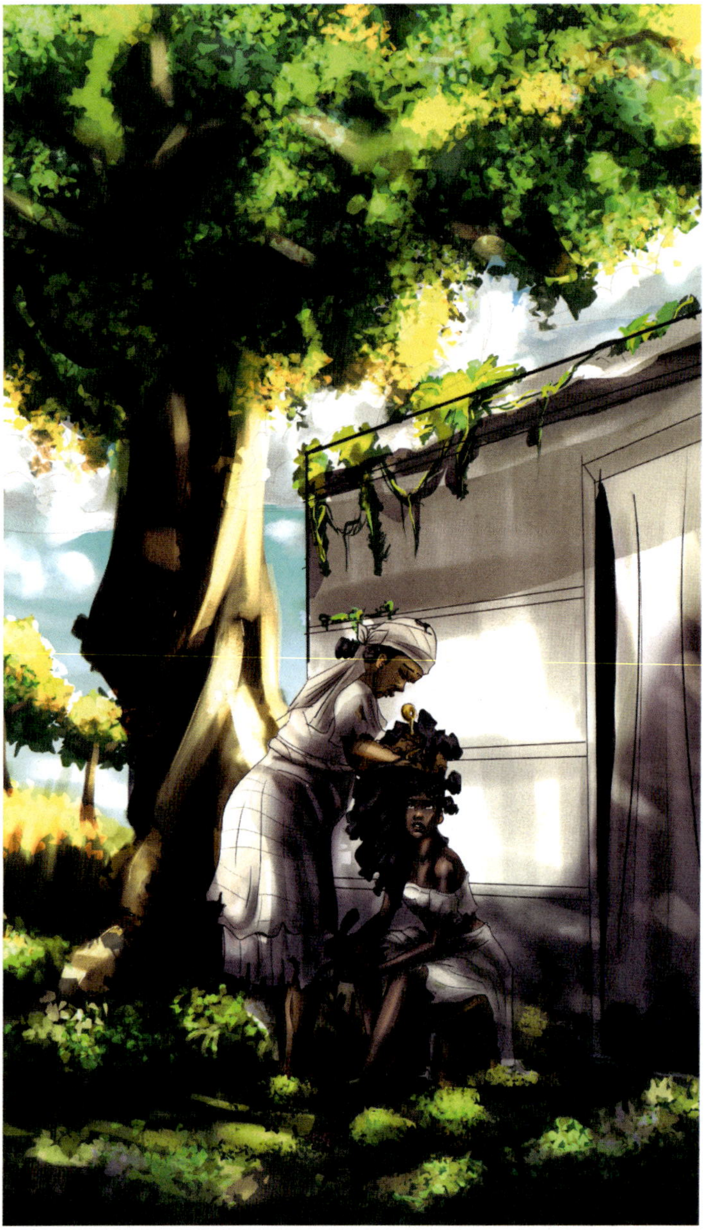

The New Land

Many days and nights went by while the ship was sailing toward an unknown destination. Some were dark and gray, while others showed a blue sky. One day Sapali woke up, and she felt the sun on her skin. She felt like she had lost track of time and had no idea how long they had been sailing. It seemed like forever. Sapali heard a screeching sound, opened her eyes some more, and looked up to the sky. There were seagulls. "Here, I haven't seen birds in so long." She woke Ama, who was sleeping next to her. Hey, Ama, I see birds; this means there is land in sight." Together they looked at the green trees and how the land was getting closer and closer. It reminded Sapali of her own land, but with one major difference–there were no mountains. The new land was completely flat.

They were all summoned to get off the boat. It was such an overwhelming and chaotic moment. Some people started screaming and crying again at the sight of the New World. As they realized they would never again see the soil of the land on which they were born. Others felt relieved that they had survived the hazardous journey. But the captives were still scared as they didn't know what was about to come.

The smell of the tree leaves in the jungle was fresh compared to the sour scent on the boat. The road was unknown, and it was terrible to be on a land that reminded her so much of her own, but this was a new world. She felt homesick. What would her family think, was her mom missing her? Sobbing and crying? Now she would also turn into one of those lost people that never returned. "Or was there a way out? Could she run away, flee, hide on a boat until it returns back to her motherland?" No, that didn't seem like a real possibility. She wouldn't know how to get out of the heavy shackles. Let alone know how to overpower those *sand-faced* people. Sapali looked around: "We are with way more people than them, even though we lost many on the sea due to sickness, and some went mad. If a couple of us could get free, we could take over this big boat. But how would we sail it. And how would we know the way back?" There was no way out.

One of the slave traders who was selling humans to slave owners walked to Sapali and unshackled her. He put her on a stand, a big wooden block. From up there, Sapali saw a big group of the same white *sand-faced* people she had come to know on the ship. But these ones had even stranger clothes on. They were slave owners, and it looked like she was going to be traded to them. Some slave owners were looking intimidating, but one was grinning from ear to ear. Sapali's clothing, a beautiful, colorful *kente* dress, was removed and replaced with a simple, white cloth. It was a stark contrast with Sapali's colorful *kente* dress that still looked well-kept even after the long journey, as her Ashanti tribe was known for high-quality fabrics. But the clothes she needed to change into looked dirty and had stains everywhere. "Do these people even wash their clothes? Why would I show myself in this?" Sapali was a young woman who loved fashion. The brighter the colors, the better. She often had attention from the boys and young men in her village. They were looking at her but careful to approach her. She had a fiery and mysterious personality. Her gracious long legs and hourglass-shaped figure made her easy on the eye. She was petite but strong, had a pretty face, and beautiful dark brown skin. Her physique and strong presence caught the attention of one of the slave owners. He had made the highest bid, and Sapali was taken along with a group of captives she didn't know very well.

As they took off, Sapali looked behind her and saw the *Apintieman* who had been communicating with her so lovely with his drumming rhythms. Suddenly, her heart stopped as she noticed they were pulled into different directions. He was brought to another place than she was. Sapali yelled but didn't even know his name. It caused a stir as he looked back at her as well and wanted to resist the slave trader. Suddenly Sapali heard a large sound and a loud scream that went through her bones. To her dismay, she saw how he was being lashed with big whips by many *sand-faced* men. He screamed as the lashes went deep into his flesh. She saw blood everywhere and screamed and cried as she was being shoved by the slave owners to walk in the direction they ordered. They locked eyes one more time as she was being led away from him. Sapali continued crying silently. The only person who had been giving her a sense of safety, her protector from a distance, was ripped away from her.

The road was long, and it seemed never-ending. They walked through sand roads and mud and saw many big green trees. Sapali didn't know where they would end up. She was just exhausted. Not only of the journey on the boat but especially being ripped away from the only person she had a sense of safety with, Sapali felt deeply depressed and hurt. Ama was in the same group as her but walked all the way in the back. She missed talking to her friend. They had connected as if they were long-lost sisters. Sapali had always wanted a sister. Ama was the only one she felt comfortable with being herself.

After a couple of days of walking, tired and hungry, the group arrives at a strange place. There are people working in the fields. It looks like they are farming. The atmosphere is very daunting as the people on the fields look very sad and fatigued. Some of them cannot even stand on their feet and are being lashed with the same big whip they had used on the man that declared his love for her. Sapali gets furious thinking about how she and her *Apintieman* were ripped apart like that. Would he still be alive? She did a quick prayer to let the ancestor protect him.

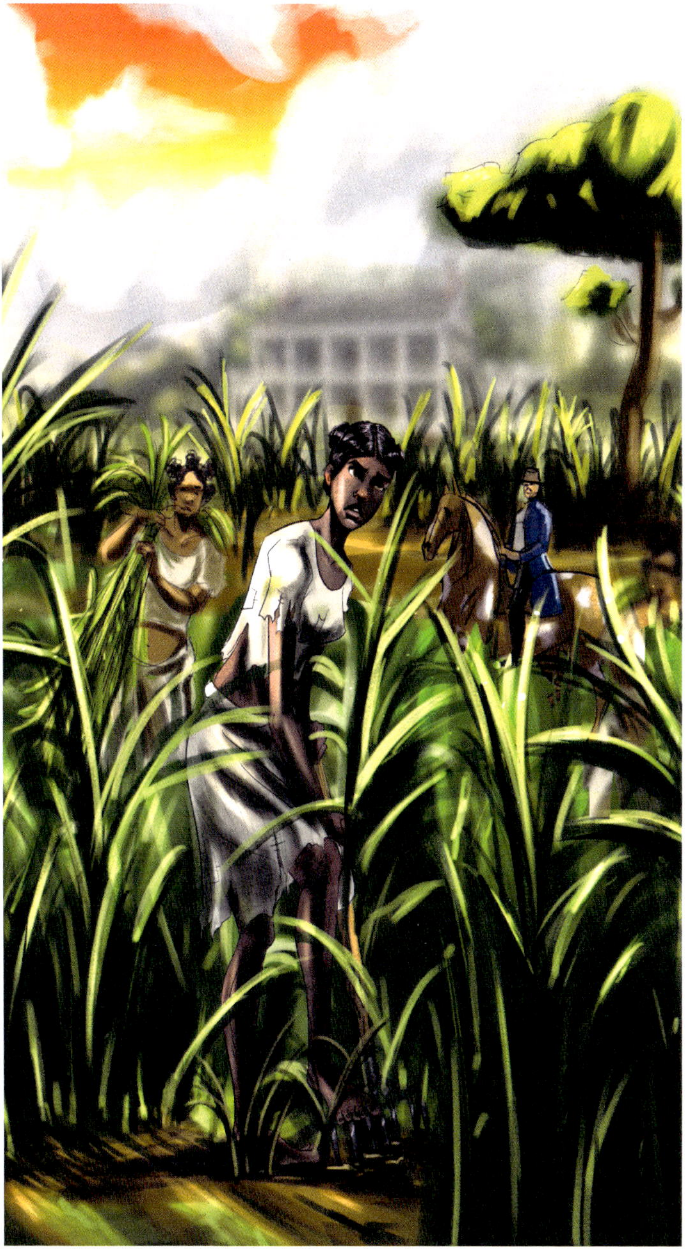

Upon arrival, Sapali looks surprised as this is the first time she also sees that there are *sand-faced* women. They wore these big skirts that looked like the upside-down shape of a calabash. Their clothes completely covered them from head to toe. "It's very hot here, just like it was on the beach before she entered the ship. How could this white tribe stand the heat?"

The group in which she arrived separated into smaller groups. She was brought to a place on the field where they were farming. Sapali was greeted by an older woman and a man. Both looked like her. The man spoke in a dialect she couldn't really understand, but she soon noticed that he ordered all people who had just arrived to follow the older woman to the field.

The older woman had beautiful deep dark brown skin, and she had *kokoti* on her face. Sapali had seen these *kokoti* often. They were markings made with a knife drenched in fire and then applying it on the face, neck, belly or any other area that wants to be accentuated. The people of her tribe used to make these marks for beauty, sometimes for protection against evil eyes, and also for strength. The older woman's look was stern yet broken. The woman reminded Sapali of the strength of her mother and grandmother. She introduced herself as Ma-Akoeba and looked around at all the lost souls that had been ripped away from their birthland —just as she herself had been many harvests ago. Ma-Akoeba looked a little longer at Sapali than the others. There was a sense of pity in her eyes, like she was sad to see another beautiful young daughter of Africa being abducted to this place of despair.

Ma-Akoeba, briefly showed Sapali how to work in the field. Sapali soon learned that the place where she was was called a plantation. They were farming sugar, coconut, and tobacco. She learned that there were many plantations like hers where they kept people from her homeland captive. The plantation Sapali was stationed at was named 'Amsterdam' and was laying at the Perica creek. On plantation Amsterdam, they had to produce as much as possible for the *sand-faced* people. There was a hierarchy on the plantation. There were overseers or *basiyas*; those were the ones who looked like her. They were African captives as well, but they had an agreement with the *sand-faced* slave owners and used their whips to beat their own people.

Life on a plantation in the Dutch Guyanas in 1722 was harsh and demanding for African captives. They were used as slaves and would toil away under the hot tropical sun. They worked long hours cutting, planting and harvesting sugarcane, coffee, cotton and other agricultural crops, as well as doing manual labor such as constructing buildings and keeping up the plantation grounds. The overseers, also known as basiyas, and the slave owners would watch their slaves very closely, making sure they kept up with their pace and productivity.

Sapali was shocked to see how they treated the people on the plantation. Some were lashed so many times the blood gushed out of their backs, and they couldn't even walk straight anymore from the pain. Still, they were forced to work. Sapali was working in the hot sun all day, and if she didn't work fast enough, she would be hit with the lash or worse. "How can this be a way to live?" She remembered she still had the rice grains in her hair that she had taken from the ship. When they were examining her, the slave owners had not discovered them. By night Sapali, piece by piece, plucked the rice grains out of her hair. It was a little hand of rice. These were original rice grains, and at this moment, it was the only thing from her homeland that she still had. "I need to hide these grains; I will need them when I can finally escape."

On the plantation, there was a mix of people from various tribes. They all spoke different languages, and it was sometimes difficult to communicate with one another. The slaves weren't allowed to talk to each other, so during hard work, they sang to communicate messages. There was always one person who took the lead voice, often Ma-Akoeba and the rest of the women repeated as a choir. Sapali knew this style of singing from back home, and it made her feel stronger. Even though her arms were trembling and her legs were shaking so much from being on her feet from dawn till dusk. Most days, it felt like every part of her body could just break. The only thing that kept her going was the singing and her thoughts of escaping this place. She remembered the sounds of the man on the ship. She had developed a keen interest in him and often daydreamed of him. It was like she could sometimes even hear his music from a distance... But that wouldn't be possible, would it?

Ma-Akoeba became like a guardian for Sapali. She grew fond of her and learned to speak Ma-Akoeba's language very quickly. Ma-Akoeba was surprised at how quickly Sapali picked up languages. During one of the many times that Ma-Akoeba was braiding Sapali's hair. The hairstyle she did for Sapali was called *pito*. Her hair was combed to the back with a partition in the middle, with two cornrow braids on each side of her head. It was a hairstyle that made it easy for her to work all day in the hot sun and kept her huge hair in place. Ma-Akoeba said: "You are a very smart girl. You see the world in a different way. I see the fire in your eyes. You are someone with knowledge, although you are still young, and you have a long way to go. I wish you a long life because people here on the plantation mostly only make it 7 to 8 years. This is the way the white men are counting harvests. They talk about years, but we just count each harvest." Sapali was always learning something new from Ma-Akoeba. It made her feel like a sense of family that she found a woman that could teach her. Even though Ma-Akoeba was not her mother, her grandmother, or her aunt, she felt like family. Ma-Akoeba told Sapali many stories about the slaves that had arrived before her. After hearing Sapali's story, Ma-Akoeba told Sapali that the people who were taken before her even had it worse. They were packed like cargo in the slave cabins. They chained them, and they had to lay down; they couldn't move or stand up to go poop and pee. They all had to do it in the place where they were lying. As you can imagine, many died of sickness and were thrown overboard. The slaves that were protesting to eat were fed anyway, by forcing open their jaws and forcing food into them. After hearing that, she shivered, but she didn't feel better. To Sapali, better off were the ones who could still smell the fresh scent of her homeland.

Sapali knew the seasons well. She saw that the rainy seasons were almost similar to her homeland. She had learned that this land in the New World was called *The Guyanas*. In this new world, they were cruel, they didn't care for people, and there was no family structure and no village head. Only slave owners and the *basiyas* were the confidants of the slave owners. The slave owners were *sand-faced* people, but the *basiyas* looked like us. They were promised better treatment if they would hit us, the ones working the fields. We are doing the hard work while they beat and whip us until we throw up from agony. Sapali felt resentment toward them.

"How could they do this to their own people? Even though this is a terrible situation, they still have a choice!" She longed for her 'old world' more and more each day and often thought about finding manners to escape, to just run away. '*Lowe,*' her friend Ama had been saying. Ama was the only one she trusted enough to discuss the idea of getting away from this place. If the *basiya* would even get a hint of them wanting to escape, Sapali would be in big trouble. Even exchanging looks with other slaves or looking in the direction of the jungle had to be done carefully. The *basiya* expected us to keep our eyes on our fieldwork at all times. It was not allowed to even think about escaping, let alone speak about it.

CHAPTER 3

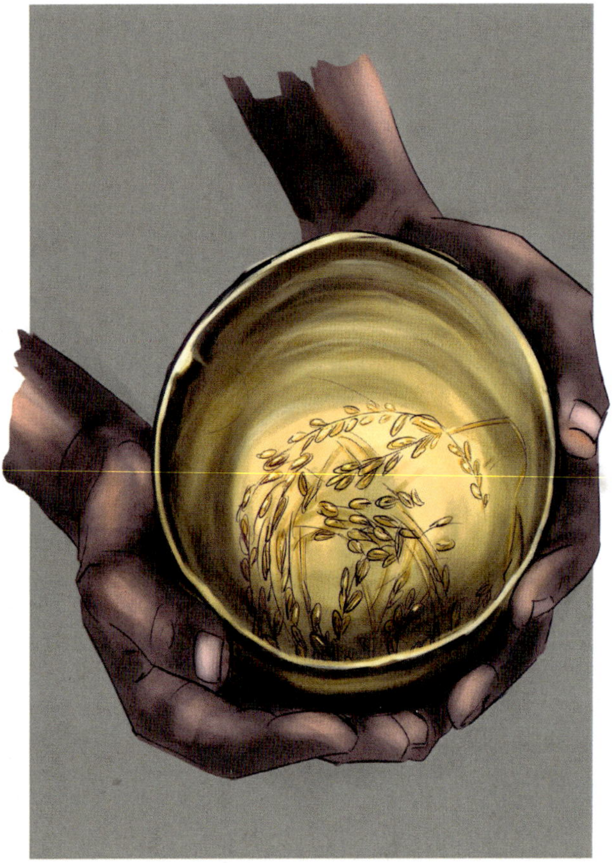

An Ingenious Plan

The position of the sun showed that it was already midday. Sapali's back was hurting as she was plowing the field. She had always been a hardworking girl back in her motherland, but this was not like anything she had ever done. She was exhausted. From early morning till late at night, they were being put to work on the plantation.

Sapali used to have great variation in her hairstyles back in her village in Africa. It complemented her beauty, and she had thick hair. It was pointing proudly to the sky, and her hair was her pride. Braiding her hair was one of the only things Sapali looked forward to in this new life. Being with Ma-Akoeba reminded Sapali about how her mother used to braid her hair back in her village… It seemed such a long time ago like she was thinking about another lifetime. The more time passed, the more difficult it got to even remember her own mother's face. Sapali stopped thinking about her sorrow and focussed on bringing some variation in the way she was wearing her hair. Under these unbearable circumstances, familiar things like braiding her hair were essential to keep her sane. Other than that, it also helped Sapali to spend some one-on-one time with Ma-Akoeba, from whom she always learned new things. Sometimes Sapali learned new languages, which herbal medicines to use when there was sickness, and how to pray to the ancestors. Ma-Akoeba often ended her prayer with the saying *Gado-afisie*, meaning that she let God lead the way. It gave Sapali such a sense of peace, so she started using it as an ending to her prayers as well. It meant that everything was ultimately all in the hands of the higher powers.

Sapali was sitting in front of Ma-Akoeba as the older woman was braiding her hair. Although Sapali had often tried to carefully propose the idea of escaping to Ma-Akoeba, the older woman had always been against it. Sapali felt that Ma-Akoeba had become too submissive. Ma-Akoeba said: "I don't have any energy left to try to escape this madness. Many people have tried, and the consequences were beyond horrific." Sapali was curious and prodded, "What happened?" Ma-Akoeba sighed deeply, nodded her head slowly, and said that she did not want to talk about it.

Sapali carefully tried to ask another question to break the silence: "Ma-Akoeba, How old are you?" Ma-Akoeba was quiet for a bit while braiding Sapali's hair more firmly. Sapali felt like she had asked the wrong question and already regretted asking. But Ma-Akoeba broke her silence and explained: "I don't know my exact age anymore. By the time I came here, I was already a mother of a kid as old as you, Sapali. However, I am not sure. The days and nights are blurry to me; so many things have happened in my life since being here. I stopped tracking time a long time ago. Every day could be our last anyway." Sapali listened carefully as Ma-Akoeba kept braiding her hair. Sapali's curiosity was bigger than her shyness. She asked Ma-Akoeba another question: "Do you have any children?" Sapali promptly felt a deep sadness coming from Ma-Akoeba. Ma-Akoeba answered swiftly: "My children have been sold to another plantation. I don't know if they are even alive. All I can do is pray that they still are and have a better life than me."

Sapali prodded: "Why didn't you try…–*she hesitated but continued as she needed to know*–why didn't you try to escape and look for them?" There are many ways we can get away. I have been counting the days and looking at the position of the sun, and I know… Ma-Akoeba stopped Sapali in the middle of her rant and said: "Let me tell you the story of a man named Kunta. Kunta was working in the same fields as you. He was a strong man, but you couldn't see it in his physique. He had long, lean muscles like you and was very fast. Those brutes chased him with their dogs into the woods. He was outrunning them, even the dogs; that's how fast he was. But you know these big long cannons that the *basiyas* and slaveholders hold in their hands? It's like they are shooting fire. Sapali nodded nervously. Ma-Akoeba continued: They shot iron bullets, and they pierced through Kunta's flesh… They captured him and took him back to this plantation. He was already severely injured and could not walk anymore. Still, the slave owners gave Kunta a punishment called *Bokoe*. This means that they bound his hands together and squeezed his knees between his arms, and put a stick between the arms and the raised knees. The stick was then firmly fixed in the ground. In this position, you can't resist. The *basiyas* struck him with a tamarind rod —until they beat him raw. No… and then they were not done. They turn Kunta around and give him the same punishments on the other side of his body." Sapali had heard of the punishment; she had never been up close when it happened. But she could hear the screams when yet again, another of her fellow Africans was being slaughtered. It was unbearable to hear. Sapali saw the horror in Ma-Akoeba's eyes as she told the story. Sapali could tell Ma-Akoeba had witnessed it, and probably Kunta was someone who had been very close to her. After a moment of silence, Sapali said to Ma-Akoeba bravely: "This is the exact reason why we need to escape! Why should we bare this much pain? How much longer can we take this?"

Ma-Akoeba continued, "Sapali, I know that you're thinking about escaping; if you do, go for it. You need to run far away from here until you reach the dense jungle. The bushes here are very low, and you can be easily traced by the bloodhounds, so I would need to help you with something to distract them." Ma-Akoeba continued: "I don't want you to be caught, and I cannot bear the thought of losing you. You're too bright of a spirit, too smart of a young woman. We are losing a lot of our people already, so many fall sick, die of sorrow, homesickness, or because of the punishments. But I can see in your eyes that your mind is set on escaping." Sapali became quiet. She looked in the distance at the little candles that were burning in the main house where the *sand-faced* people lived... The slaves had to sleep together outside in this small barn. Ma-Akoeba continued braiding Sapali's hair in silence. She was almost done.

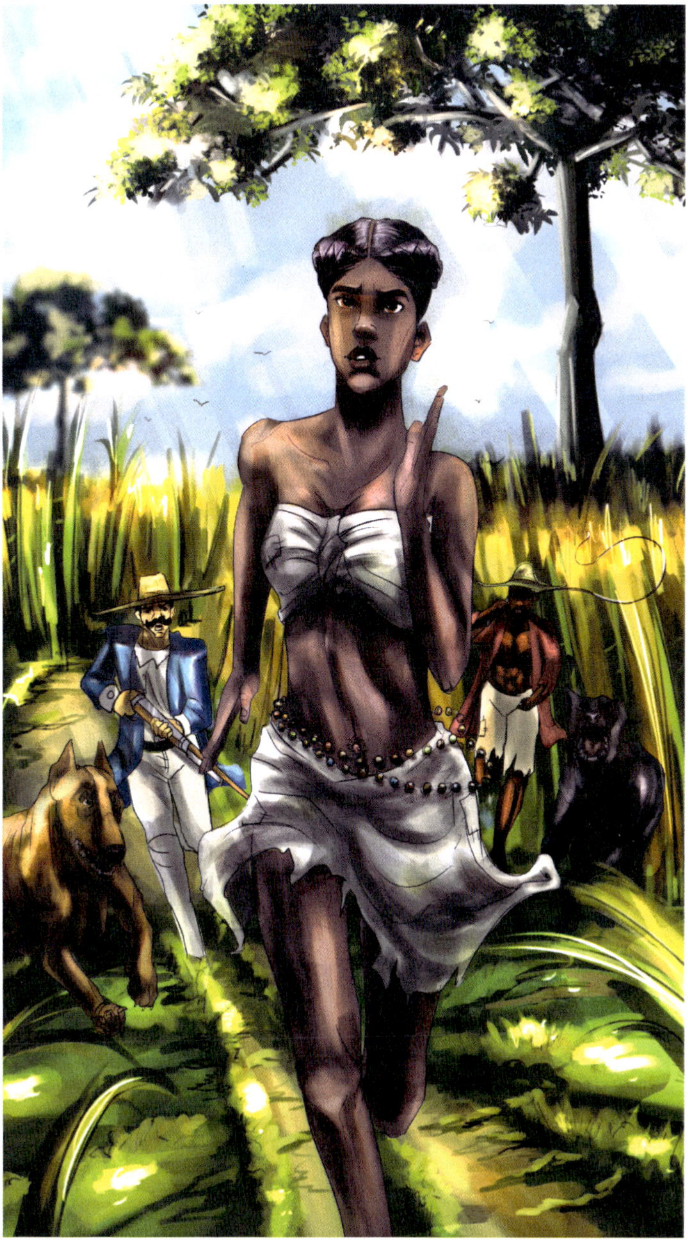

The thought of freedom kept Sapali occupied. Every day when she was working in the fields, she looked around and tried to strategize various scenarios to escape. The jungle was right in front of her, and it looked like it was impossible to penetrate. That's how dense the trees were, let alone all the animals that were there lurking in the high grass. She had seen many poisonous snakes, frogs, those little crocodiles called *caiman*, and even jaguars also known as *boeboe*, from time to time. While working on the plantations, Sapali felt freedom was right in front of her, yet it seemed unattainable.

"We are so close to freedom. We can almost taste it." Sapali said to Ama while cutting the sugar canes. Ama replied: "I know, and we should definitely make a run for it. I also talked to two other girls about escaping." Sapali looked frightened: "Are you sure they will not tell on us? This is risky!" Sapali started walking around nervously. Ama reassured Sapali: "No, don't worry. They won't tell on us because they are practically the same person, Ama said with a cheeky smile. You've seen them often, the twins Josenki and Abentiba. Both of them have been plotting an escape but are ready to join us if we have a plan." Ama continued, "I know Sapali that you have been observing and strategizing many options to escape. You don't talk much, but I see the way you stare into the distance. Your mind is constantly analyzing the best way to leave. You are very smart and see-through things. I truly believe our best chances are to flee in a group. Most people try to escape alone, but they don't last..." Sapali thought back to the stories of Ma-Akoeba that served as warnings—especially the story of why Kunta had failed to escape. Sapali did not want to make the same mistake, to escape from plantation Amsterdam and starve in the jungle or get injured by dangerous insects and poisonous plants. If the slave owners would catch them in the woods with their big scary bloodhounds and rifles, especially the bloodhounds, the consequences would be terrible. When people flee alone, the chances of their survival are slim. Ma-Akoeba had told her. Sapali had heard many wise words from Ma-Akoeba, one of them that stuck with her the most was: "Freedom is like a *Kankantrie*; one person's arm cannot embrace it."

While Sapali was working in the field, she kept thinking about Ma-Akoeba's words. She knew Ma-Akoeba meant that Sapali's best chances of survival were to not escape alone. The conversation with Ama was also constantly on Sapali's mind. She trusted Ama. Ama was like a sister to her. But can she trust the twins? Escaping with a group posed risks as well. Maybe they could help set up a diversion. They had to distract the *basiyas* somehow 'cause even at night, he was looking at them. Those brutes never slept. The advantage of being with a group is that you can delegate tasks and work as one. Trust is the most important ingredient to succeed. Sapali thought to herself: *"Maybe I should ask Ama to have a meeting with the twin? I have to take this risk and see how we can make it work."*

From a distance, Sapali heard Ama sing. The song was a familiar song to Sapali as Ama was singing to her in code language about where they would meet up that night. One of the few forms of motivation on the plantations was the rhythms of drumming and singing that they would employ while they worked. Inspired by their African homeland, the slaves used these rhythms and singing to push themselves through the long hours of hard labor, giving them a sense of belonging, home, and unity. That night she met up with Ama and the twins Josenki and Abentiba. There were many women on the plantation. But next to Ma-Akoeba, who became like a mother figure to her, Ama was the only young woman Sapali was closest to. Ama made many friends on the plantation. Sapali was a little bit more reserved. She just wanted to stay focussed on how to get away from the place. Having too many relationships with people meant she had to also bear the pain when one of them perished. Losing people had become too painful for her. So Sapali often kept her distance and had a quiet demeanor about her. Still, she had a passionate desire for freedom burning within her.

Josenki looked at Sapali, and Sapali sized them both up. Are they ready for the task? They seemed so small and so petite. But that could also be an advantage. Sapali saw that the twins had strong legs; their thighs were big, and they had both nice round bottoms. She knew the guys in her village would love a physique like this. Sapali had a more twiglike figure, she was also athletic and had toned arms and legs, but she was tall and lean. They must be good runners, Sapali thought to herself. Abentiba started speaking. She was probably the vocal one of the two. Josenki and I were planning to escape. We already timed for several weeks when the guards are usually off their posts. There is a little gap in-between where they switch guards. In order to further prevent slaves from running away, the plantation owners would post guards at the perimeter of the plantations to keep an eye out for any potential escapees. They would also employ well-trained guard dogs to help track down any runaways. As Abentiba explained how to make use of their limited window of opportunity, Josenki interrupted nervously. "What will we do about the guard dogs? They can smell us and sense small movements from a long distance." Sapali already had an idea of how to distract the guard dogs. She would need Ma-Akoeba's help for it, though. Sapali calmed Josenki down and said, "Don't worry, I have something for that." Let's meet up again tomorrow night to plan everything out. Agreed?

The next day Sapali was harvesting tobacco. This soil seemed to be as fertile as the one back home. Only the color of the soil in her homeland was different. There it was more reddish, and here it was brown. By sunset, she got startled as she heard a lot of commotion. People were yelling, and she saw slave owners with their guard dogs and rifles running into the jungle. She started trembling; she couldn't help but fear for the ones who had tried to escape. She prayed within herself and asked the ancestors to protect them. To calm her nerves, she ended her prayer by saying *Gado-afisie* and started singing a song out loud. It was a lullaby her grandmother used to sing to her when she was a little girl. To her surprise, the other women caught up with her, and together, they sang. Their voices were powerful and reached far. It gave them the strength to push through, and they worked even harder than before.

As time passed by, she heard people shouting in the distance. The sounds of their rifles and the loud and wild barking of the dogs came closer. Soon she saw that a group of three field slaves that were working close to her had tried to escape. They failed miserably as they were caught, two males and one female. During her time at the plantation, she had never experienced a whole group of slaves being caught. The slaves started crying as they saw their fellow people on the plantation. Sapali saw that one of the escapees' leg was ripped apart by the guard dogs. His flesh was barely hanging onto the bone, and he was screaming his lungs out. The other two were pulled by a rope around their neck as they resisted crying and screaming. They were about to be punished heavily and received so many whips from the *basiya* it seemed to last forever. The one with the scattered leg kept screaming out of extreme pain and abruptly became frighteningly quiet. He had probably passed out from the pain or worse. His head was slightly tilted to one side as the *basiya* kept whipping his lifeless body. Sapali looked at the back of his head but quickly withdrew her gaze to avoid having to see more of this horrific scene. The harsh and demanding work from sunrise to sunset, with limited breaks in-between for much-needed rest, made people weak. Finding a way to escape and getting caught with severe punishment. That can be too much to bear for even the strongest among us. Sapali cried silently, and so did the women and men around her. All slaves on the plantation were obliged to watch as their people were punished to death.

It took a couple of days before Sapali dared to think about escaping again. She had been numb and tried to get through the days. The image of the slaughter had stayed vividly in her mind. Ama tried to make eye contact with her for days. But she ignored it for the most part. One day Ama came to her while they were working in the high grass, and she said: "Sapali, I need to tell you something." And she pointed at her belly. I am pregnant. They made me have intercourse with a man I completely dislike. They want more people to work on the plantation, and they breed us like they do with their dogs.

We are not animals! Ama whispered angrily. They will do the same to you as they want to do with most of the young women here. We have to escape and fast! Soon I won't be as fast or able to run again. Sapali felt like her stomach had turned upside down. Ama pregnant? And she was about to have the same happen to her? No way.

That night the 3 girls met again in secret. This time it had become even more dangerous. With the traumatic experience still in their head, they were all trembling. Sapali plotted with the girls to come up with a diversion technique. To make sure that they have multiple options. No matter what, they need to succeed. After the quick meeting, she went to her plantation mother, Ma-Akoeba. Sapali said: "This may be the last time that I will see you, Ma-Akoeba," her voice was trembling. Ma-Akoeba looked at her in silence: "I know you will be trying to escape. I had a dream about it, and the ancestors guided me to tell you: *If you want to go quick, you can go alone, but if you want to go far, you go together.*" It was an African proverb that Sapali had heard before, but she was a bit confused: "Ma-Akoeba, you won't stop me?" Ma-Akoeba answered: "I won't. Instead, I have something to help you succeed." Ma-Akoeba left and came back with a little flask; there was a substance in it. "What is this?" Sapali asked. "Sssshhh...!" Ma-Akoeba whispered. She quietly started smearing the substance over Sapali's arms, legs, chest, and face, ended with her hand on Sapali's forehead, and started praying. After the prayer, Ma-Akoeba explained to Sapali what the substance was made of. It was a collection of wild herbs from the plantation and a unique combination of ground tobacco and coconut oil. Sapali noted the peculiar odor that it emitted. To Sapali, this discovery was something special – she called it *'Obiya'*. Ma-Akoeba said that when Sapali smeared it on her body and clothes, the odor would prevent the dogs from tracking or tracing her when she escaped. But they still had to perfect it. As an eager apprentice, the young slave girl Sapali became involved in creating better versions of the potion. Hours and days passed as Ma-Akoeba and Sapali worked together to perfect their technique of employing Obiya to prevent new dogs from sniffing them out. Before Sapali walked away, Ma-Akoeba firmly embraced her and said: "Remember, herbs are the leaves of life."

The discovery of *Obiya* was shared with the twins and Ama. The four girls decided to also have two men involved with their escape. Kwaku and Kofi were cousins and also had a strong connection. They had survived so far but deemed their chance of survival becoming slimmer as each day passed. They wanted out just like the girls. Sapali knew they would need men. She had a vision to set up a village outside of this plantation. Where they could live in freedom and peace. The men could take care of the construction of houses and create ditches and drainage systems for farming. So the water could reach the plants. Sapali had carefully observed on the plantation that this was men's work. The planting of the seeds in the ground was mostly done by women, while both men and women engaged in harvesting. Sapali thought about Ama's condition. They didn't have much time left. We have to leave before she truly shows. Women who gave birth on the plantation had only a couple of days to feed their children. Recovery time was slim as within two weeks, they had to return to the gruesome work in the fields. Elderly women like Ma-Akoeba had to then take over care of the babies, while the young mothers worked tirelessly from early mornings to late nights.

Sapali more frequently heard drums in the distance. Were they from another plantation nearby on the other side of the impenetrable jungle? Or were these people perhaps free? She got excited thinking about the possibility of runaway slaves being out there. Living in freedom. Some of them must have outsmarted the slaveholders. "Even though it's dangerous, I know with the help of our ancestors, we can make it. Let's follow the drums."

CHAPTER 4

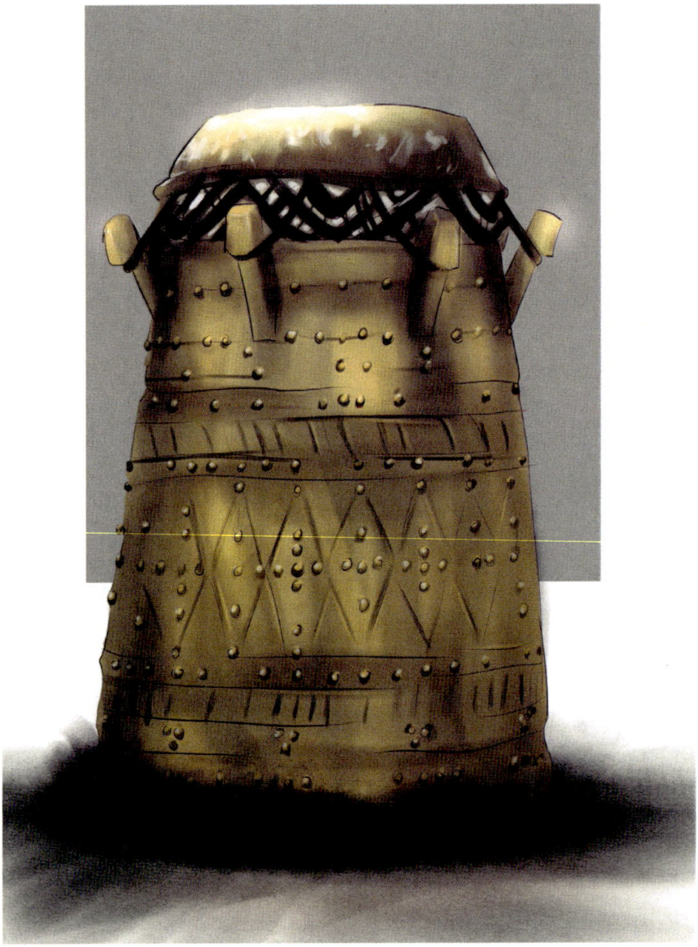

Escape To Where?

It was almost time to go. Sapali and her five confidants held their last meeting before the escape. Ama, in her delicate condition, the twins, Josenki and Abentiba, and cousins, Kwaku and Kofi, all looked at Sapali with trust. They all looked up to her as she had a vision for life beyond this place. The nightmare might finally be over. Sapali was calm, yet she exuded authority.

The suspense in the room was high. The stakes were tremendous as they were now strategizing how to distract the *basiya*. They were a little worried if the aromatic Obja brew would really work. There was no other way to try. The price of failure was high, and they were running the risk of being tortured to death. Still, the prospect of Freedom was more alluring than ever. The ways of the slave owners and *basiyas* were getting worse and worse. It had already been unbearable to work on the plantation. But it seemed like with every escape attempt by the slaves on the plantation, the punishments became worse. Josenki asked Sapali if it would be possible to take the older woman along. "Out of all of us, you are closest to her. Then we could be sure that her spiritual power is helping us as well." Sapali wanted nothing more than to take Ma-Akoeba along. It would help them with life after the plantation. Sapali couldn't imagine leaving the plantation without Ma-Akoeba as they grew so close. But she also knew how protective Ma-Akoeba was. She was a mother figure to Sapali.

Later that evening, Sapali entered the shed where Ma-Akoeba normally braided her hair. To her surprise, Ma-Akoeba was nowhere to be found. All the bottles with herbs that Ma-Akoeba stored had been broken. Glass was shattered all over the floor. Sapali looked more closely in the dark and saw there was blood on the wooden bench where she always sat down to get her hair braided. Sapali was in shock and felt in her stomach that something was terribly wrong.

Hastily she made her way to the barn where all the slaves slept. She gently shook Ama awake and told her what she had seen. Ama's eyes got big, and her expression changed to extreme worry. "Sapali, we need to leave now; we can't risk another night." Sapali agreed, but the diversion had to be set up first if they wanted a chance to outrun the guard dogs and the slave owners with their rifles. "Kwaku and Kofi are sleeping on the other side of the plantation, and we can't send a message to them now. If we start singing at this late hour, the *basiyas* will notice that there is something going on," Sapali whispered to Ama. Suddenly, Sapali breaks down. She had never done this in front of anyone to see. All night Ama held Sapali close to her while she cried against her chest. There were no tears left. But all Sapali could do was cry silently while staring into the darkness of the bush near them.

It seemed daybreak arrived faster than ever. Work on the field was about to start. Sapali already heard the *basiyas* screaming and using their whips to force slaves to work. She had not slept, and she sneaked by the Ma-Akoeba's shed and peeked inside. Desperately hoping that she would see the familiar face of the woman who became her family. Again there was no one, and the shattered glass that she had seen the night before was cleaned up. Sapali was shocked to see that her bench was gone. She always sat there while Ma-Akoeba braided her hair. It was the only place where she could feel a bit at home. They had so many meaningful conversations there. Sapali touched her hair and closed her eyes. She could see Ma-Akoeba's face.

While laboring on the plantation grounds, Sapali covertly looked around to see if there was any sign of her. Suddenly, the slave master and their wives came out of their houses. The men had long white robes on, and were holding weird-looking wooden objects and a book in their hands. They looked like spiritual objects but were different from the ones she knew. They were angrily waving up the objects in the air, and were saying something in their own language. Sapali had learned to speak Dutch; this was the language of the slave owners. Ma-Akoeba had taught her in secret, so she understood most of what they were saying. The slave master held one of the glass bottles of Ma-Akoeba "We found this, and from now on, there will be no more use of your magic," he said with a shrill voice. The slave owners said that from now on, the slaves were not allowed to do any herbal mixtures for healing or magic. They would need to convert to the religion of the slave owners and renounce their Gods. If they were caught with any herbal or medicinal craft, they would get the *Bokoe* punishment for 7 days. Some others also understood the slave owner's language and seemed disturbed. Many of the ailments they all got from the physically excruciating work were healed by their own herbal medicines. The advantage of this new land was that there were many herbs that they didn't even have in their homeland. And step by step Ma-Akoeba had been teaching Sapali about how to make the various remedies.

The slave master continued, and this time, he raised his voice: "If we catch you with any type of heathen practice, you will disappear just like the slave everyone knew as Ma-Akoeba." When he mentioned Ma-Akoeba's name, Sapali lost her breath. Her heart started beating faster, and she panicked. She wanted to scream just as she had seen the mothers do, who had been separated from their children when they were sold off to other plantations. The mothers stamped their feet frantically and rolled on the ground screaming out to their sons and daughters while the *basiyas* restrained them. The children's facial expressions showed a mixture of confusion, deep grief, and hopelessness as they were pulled away from them. Crying out loud, knowing they would never see their mothers again. She could relate to the pain in the hearts of the children as they were brutally separated from their mothers. Ma-Akoeba was like a mother to her. And now she would never see her again.

The slaves who understood the slave owners' language needed to convey the message to the rest so that their fellow captives wouldn't get in trouble. Sapali explained what the slave owner had said to Ama, the twins, and the cousins. They looked at her with amazement. They knew Sapali was intelligent, but they did not know she was this knowledgeable and even knew the slave owner's language. Sapali spoke in the – code language that the six of them had developed so that other slaves could not tell on them–and said: "Ma-Akoeba was caught with the herbs, and the *basiyas*, and the slave owners have killed her. I saw the blood on the bench and the shattered glass. We have to leave tonight." They all agreed and put their plan in motion.

Sapali and Ma-Akoeba had worked together on the *Obiya* mixture. It was the last thing they had done together. Sapali looked at the sky, and for the first time in ages, she felt a tear rolling over her cheek. She believed that she did not have any tears left; because she needed to endure so much pain, emotionally, physically, and spiritually. Ma-Akoeba had been a spiritual leader for many of the slaves. The way she took in new arrivals and taught them the unwritten rules of the plantation was impeccable. She was highly intelligent, knew many different languages, and was an excellent healer. Ma-Akoeba was like a mother and grandmother figure to all. A strong African woman, a multi-talented leader, and a healer. Now Ma-Akoeba has become an ancestor.

Before they were ready to leave, Sapali went to her secret place behind the barn. She dug up the bottle with the *Obiya* mixture. She had hidden the mixture after brewing it at Ma-Akoeba's place. Sapali was inconsolable. She did not even have a chance to say goodbye to her dear Ma-Akoeba. In a piece of white cloth, she found the rice grains that she carefully had hidden in her hair while being on the ship. It was the only thing she had left from her homeland. During the harvest on the plantation, she had also consistently sneaked some rice grains in her hair. Sapali hoped it would be enough to start a new village and attached the rice grains to her braids while she prayed on them. Ma-Akoeba was an ancestor now. Sapali prayed for the protection of herself and the others who were joining on this escape mission: "Thank you for giving us all we need at this moment. I pray you are here to guide us through. Please give us strength in our legs as well as our minds. God, walk ahead of us: *Gado-afisie.*"

Kofi and Kwaku were on the other side of the plantation and had taken branches of the big ant tree. They placed them at the spots where the *basiyas* normally sat. They made a trace of molasses, which was a by-product of sugar; it was sweet and attracted the ants. Before they knew what was happening to them, the *basiyas* would be covered with a colony of big ants, which would draw the attention of the other *basiyas* as well. With the chaos that would ensue from this, they had their chance to escape! Kofi and Kwaku were very skilled in how to capture branches full of big ants without getting bitten themselves. Everyone in the group had their purpose.

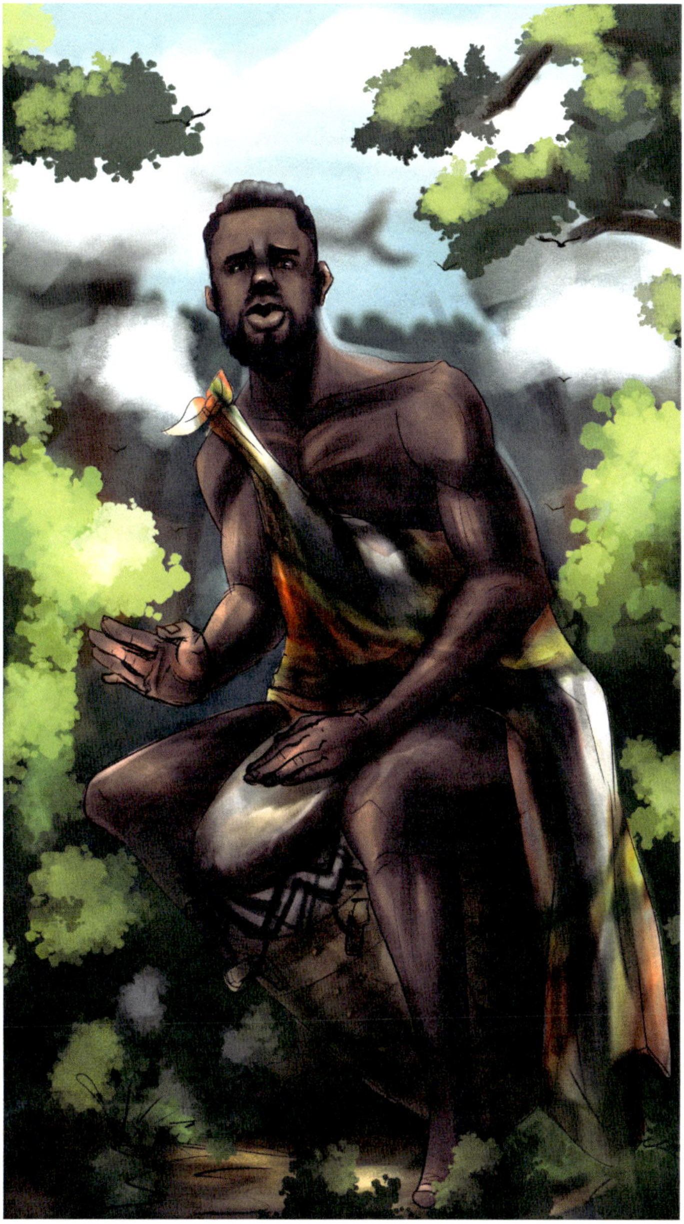

Sapali was waiting for the sign; the moment the candle lights at the slave master's house were turned off, it was time to gather at the big tree. It was their rendezvous point where they smeared the *Obiya* mixture on their body and clothes. As soon as they heard the *basiyas* on the plantation scream for help, the guards at the edge of the woods left their posts to run and see what was going on. This was their chance. "Run!" Sapali whispered as they all ran away deep into the woods towards their freedom.

It was a full moon. Sapali was running ahead, followed by Ama, the twins, and the cousins. The light of the moon guided them so they could see a little, even in the darkness caused by the close-knit trees and bushes. They need to pick up the pace to get a head start. As soon as the *basiyas* noticed that this had been a diversion, they would send their bloodthirsty dogs to follow them with rifles. The slaves were worth a lot to the plantation owners. It was free labor and allowed them to make high profits on their trades.

While running, Sapali touched her hair; she was afraid the grains would fall out. She had never had to run with the grains in her hair before, but they were still there in her braids. The grains were essential for life after the plantation. To create a village, a new community where they can live in freedom and peace. The jungle had a lot to offer, but she still needed to learn more about what seeds were edible and which were poisonous and needed to be avoided. I didn't know about the plants in this new place. They ran and ran until their knees felt weak. Sapali suddenly heard the drum, so it was real. She sometimes doubted if it really was a drumming pattern or not, as it sounded like a rumbling sound in the distance, like the sound of a thundercloud. The sound was clear, and she could anticipate from what direction it came. It was not too far from where they were. The jungle was dense; she looked behind and observed that the others also were listening carefully. They didn't understand what was being played. Sapali knew she had heard this style of drumming before. They were all startled when they suddenly heard barking in the distance. They all looked at each other in fear. Kofi said: "The *basiyas* and slave owners know we are gone and are looking for us; we have to go now!" Ama was still catching her breath; she felt dizzy. Her pregnancy and the long hard work on the plantation had made her feel weaker. Kwaku saw that Ama wasn't feeling good and said to Ama: "Come get on my back, please." They ran and ran, but the dogs were catching up to them. All six captives were running towards their freedom while being hurt by thorns and leaves hitting their faces as they increased their pace. The muscles in their legs were burning as their stamina decreased. Sapali heard Ma-Akoeba's voice in her head guiding her: "Follow the *kimonimoni* (light kevers), and you can sleep there. When you see a *kimonimoni*, it means the presence of good spirits and the absence of wild animals." Sapali saw the *kimonimoni* lighting up in the darkness and crawling up a big tree. It was a very big tree that reminded her of the God tree (*Nyame Dua*) in her homeland. Sapali remembered Ma-Akoeba telling her: "Not to sleep on the ground, only in a tree." Sapali inspected the tree and saw that the inside of the tree was hollow, so they could hide inside and climb to the top. They sat still and held their breath. They were hoping that the *Obiya* mixture truly worked. Or else the dog would sniff their scents and would know they were in the tree.

It was so dark they couldn't even see their own hands. The moonlight barely shone in the tree. They heard a little rattling down and heard footsteps and whispering. The dogs tried to sniff, but they couldn't catch their scent and couldn't locate them in the tree. Sapali thought to herself; *the Obiya potion is truly working*, she pleaded with the ancestors in her mind. "Please save us; grant us our freedom." Soon they heard the dogs and footsteps near the place where they were hidden, *basiyas*, slave owners, and their dogs walked on. It worked! Thank you Ma-Akoeba, for guiding us.

CHAPTER 5

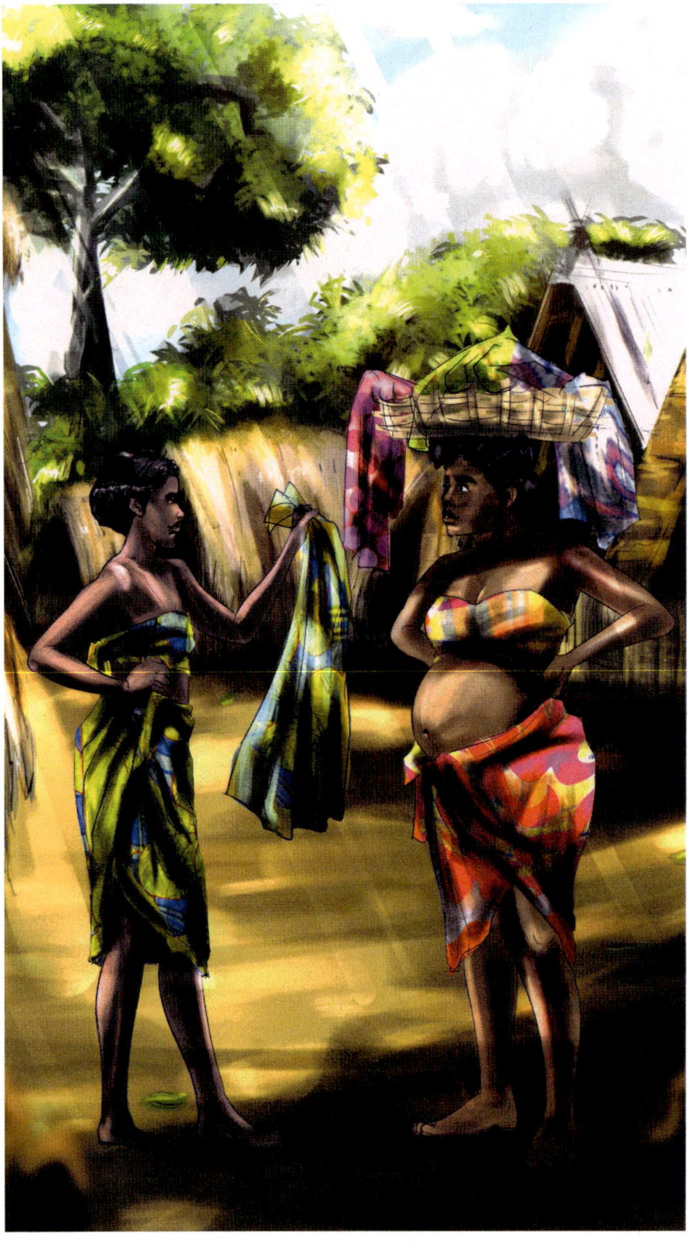

Boobiabla

Sapali suddenly woke up. She hadn't realized that she had slept. She held the trunk of the tree so tightly and never would have thought that she would be able to fall asleep in this weird position. It just showed how exhausted she was. Ama was sitting next to her and gently leaned with her head on Sapali's shoulder. Were they really free? Did they pull this off?

Sapali looked around and could not find Kwaku and Kofi. To her relief, they had already climbed out of the tree. It seemed like they were looking to catch some little animals to eat. The twins Josenki and Abentiba were also walking around and plucking fruits. They had learned the old wise saying: "If a monkey eats it, you can eat it." Everyone was exhausted and needed nutrition. Especially Ama, as a pregnant woman, needed to have food and water fast. Promptly, it started raining; it was one of those heavy rainfalls. It was as if the ancestors could hear Sapali think, and she felt a deep connection while being in the woods like this. She had a sense that everything may work out in the end. Now her first priority was to get Ama to drink. Sapali helped Ama climb out of the tree. Kofi saw the two getting out of the tree and rushed over to help Sapali with Ama. He said, "This way, go stand under this banana tree." He took a big banana tree leaf, which was almost as tall as him, and held it against Ama's lips. She drank the water as if she had never had water in her life before. All of them felt relieved while the rain was abundantly pouring over them from the sky.

Many days and nights passed as the group of six walked on to find a place to settle in freedom. Sapali thought about Ma-Akoeba often and all the advice she had given about the rainforest: "When you reach a swamp, walk around it, don't try to cross it. And when you meet a creek, walk upstream." Finding their way through the dense jungle was extremely difficult, and they were still on high alert. They couldn't run forever as Ama was with-child and needed a place to rest soon. After some days, they found a creek where they could drink water and rest for a bit. The traumatic experience of being chased by the guard dogs and the slave owners was still fresh in their minds. As the days went by, all of them were getting more talkative as they started to experience a sense of freedom. All were exchanging stories about how they had been captured and shipped out to the world they were in now. One story was even more horrific than the other. "When did you arrive on the plantation?" Kwaku asked Sapali. She answered: I arrived about one harvest ago. So compared to many, I am still pretty new." Kwaku replied: "Kofi and I have already been here for 5 harvests. I heard the ship on which you and Ama arrived was way better than ours. You could sing and drum on yours." Sapali replied: "With you, this was not the case?" Kofi stepped in: "No, the ship we arrived in we were chained and packaged so densely on top of each other. Only our ancestors have made us survive. And the fact that we have each other is a miracle as well. Many people around us died. Some starved themselves, and others found opportunities to escape by jumping off the ship."

As they were deep into their conversations, Sapali noticed a familiar sound. It was the sound of the drums again. The drumming pattern was clearer than ever, unlike the other occasions when she was on the plantation and had doubted herself. She knew she had heard it while they were escaping the plantation. Sapali spontaneously climbed into a tree near them to see which direction the sound was coming from. She was up there so fast that Ama, Josenki, Abentiba, Kwaku, and Kofi watched her climb in awe. Sapali reached the higher parts of the tree in no time. Her athletic body made it seem like an easy task, but they all knew what she did wasn't easy at all! Sapali was a strong young woman. Not only mentally but also physically. The way she sped up there was like something spiritual had taken over as Sapali heard the drums.

Up the huge tree, Sapali saw a large part of the jungle. She had never been this high ever in her life. It felt like true freedom as if she could even fly with the many colorful birds around her. She was surprised that she had got up there so fast. It's like a force had lifted her up, making it feel like she was as light as a feather. She looked around, and through the dense leaves, she saw a little open spot. It seemed as if the trees had been removed, and there were a handful of men. They were building structures that looked like the foundation of the houses back in her village. A little farther away, she saw one that was actually finished. Her heart skipped a beat. This could be it, our place of freedom! She climbed down and started to walk towards the drums and signaled the cousins Kofi and Kwaku to walk along with her. Josenki and Abentiba stayed with Ama hidden in the bushes, just to be cautious as she was not entirely sure of the intention of all the men. She walked closer and saw the man who was playing the drum. It looked like the drums that she knew from her homeland, but this one had a slightly different shape and sound. But the drumming language was the same. He was playing and saying this was a place of freedom and new beginnings. That all who hear the sound should come to them, and they will. Sapali was the first one to get out of the woods and show herself. She looked closer, and she recognized the smile. It was him! Her *Apintieman*, her protector, was still alive? How could this be? Sapali felt so happy that she automatically ran towards him. He stopped playing as he saw the elegant long legs, beautiful coco skin, and extremely happy face approach him. He recognized Sapali immediately, and they embraced passionately. Both were laughing and giggling as they touched each other's faces. It was the first time the two were able to touch each other. Finally, she could feel how his skin felt, how his strong jaw touched her cheek, and broad arms embraced her. For the first time since entering the new world, Sapali felt safe.

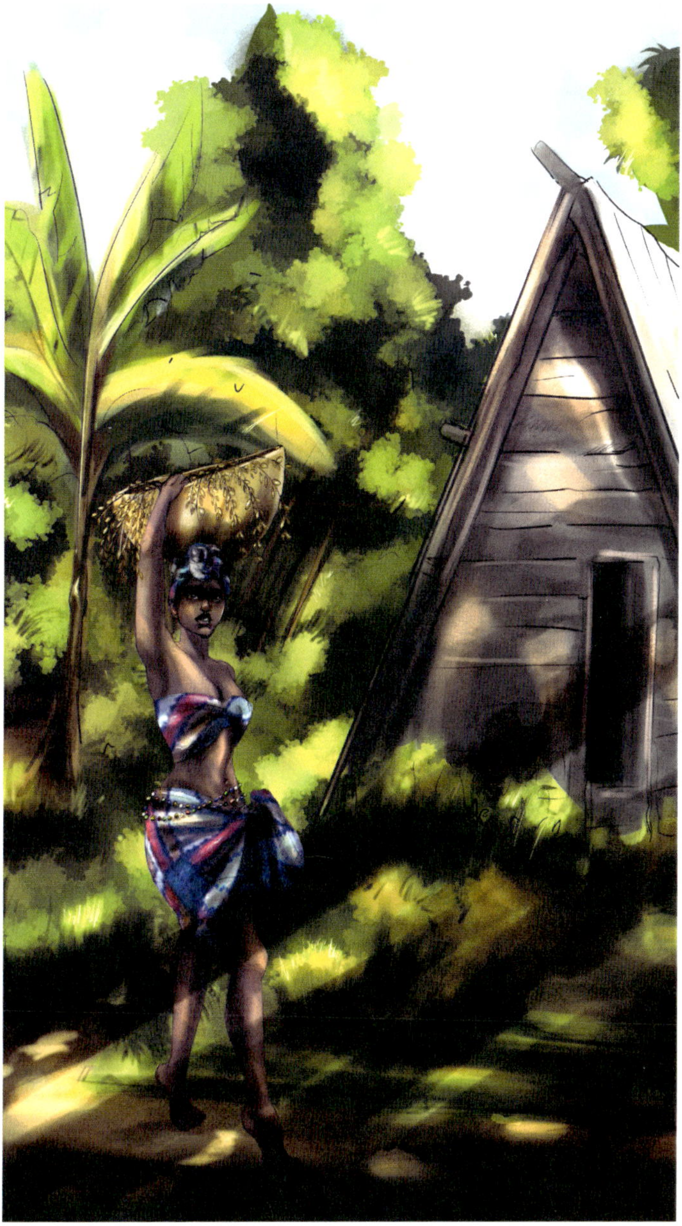

Josenki, Abentiba, and Ama came out of the woods and looked confused. They had never seen this open and carefree part of Sapali's personality. "So you know him?" Kwaku asked carefully. "Yes", Sapali answered. "He saved me from being beaten or worse when we were captured. I call him *Apintieman* as he kept our spirit high on the ship by leading the drummers and playing the *Apintie codes*." Sapali looked at the *Apintieman* and asked: "Where you the one that I heard all this time?" He said, "Yes, my love. I made the drums out of the strongest wood I could while hoping I would find you. I could feel in my heart that you were not too far away from me. However, some days I lost hope, but still, I kept talking to you with my drums. I prayed you were still alive and that you would find freedom." He picked Sapali up, spinned her around, and said: "My Queen, the ancestors never failed my prayers; they brought *you* to me." Sapali smiled from ear to ear, showing her beautiful teeth. After the long separation, Sapali and her *Apintieman* finally reunited in joy.

Later that evening, they all gathered by the campfire and ate fresh fish captured by the men. As they were happily feasting on their fresh meal, Sapali was picking her hair. After a while, she held her hand near the fire and showed everyone the rice grains in her hand. She said proudly: "This comes from our homeland. We can use this to have a new life, a village, a real community. And build back what was taken from us."

A couple of moons went by, and they established a village. Sapali and her *Apintieman* had been chosen as leaders of their community. Sapali had strategic insight and spiritual power. Her husband, the *Apintieman*, had the ability to speak in highly complex codes to communicate, to find other communities like theirs, or help free more of their people from the dreadfulness of plantation life. The rice grains Sapali had brought were immensely valuable to them. It allowed her people to farm and always have a reliable and energy rich food source. They had an excellent structure and task delegation system in their village. As the men were plowing the fields, the women were planting the grains. Rice plants grow to a height of three to four feet over an average of 120 days after planting. Sapali had been counting the days and knew the seasons well. Harvesting season was about to begin. By using sickles and knives, the women and men cut the grass stalks. The grains were removed from these stalks by 'threshing' them. This means that the edible part of the rice grain was loosened from the straw to which it is attached. Sapali and her people were slinging the stalks against the surface of a tree. The grains loosened up and fell out. Loud *Apintie drumming*, singing, and dancing ensued as their first harvest was celebrated. The rice from their homeland had allowed them to establish a home away from home.

One night all of a sudden, Sapali woke up soaked in sweat. In the woods, it was not hot during the nighttime. The trees provided a cool environment that reminded Sapali of the mountains back home. Well, she cannot call that her home anymore; now, this is her home which she created out of willpower, focus, extreme courage, and the guidance of her ancestors. She was lying next to her husband, the *Apintieman*. Sapali woke him up, and he intuitively knew something was wrong. He looked at her with eyes wide open as she whispered to him: "I had a dream. Ma-Akoeba came to me and said there were dogs and bullets chasing us. I feel it was a warning we need to go." Her husband told her that he would check on the others and tell them about her vision. He stepped outside and anxiously ran towards the houses of the others. The *Apintieman* stopped abruptly as he heard dogs barking and howling in the distance. He immediately changed direction and walked back to his home. He rushed inside and whispered frantically, "Grab the rice grains and *Obiya* mixture. They are coming. I will wake up the others now." Sapali quickly wore a *panji* and took the things her husband had told her to bring. Sapali stepped outside and went straight to Ama's house, where she stayed together with Kofi. By now, Ama was almost due and could give birth in a matter of days. It was hard for her to run now. She could get her baby at any time. Kofi and Kwaku both decided to carry her. The *Apintieman* had to leave behind his drum. They would not be able to bring it along. It was too big, too heavy and would slow them down. He had carefully crafted his drum to communicate with Sapali, who, because of it, became his wife. It was a special instrument to everyone in the village. The Apintiedrum had brought them together and united all of them in this freshly formed community. Sadly, almost everything they had built since their escape was left behind. They all were once again on the run…

Acknowledgement

We are humbled and grateful to acknowledge the people and organizations who have played a crucial role in bringing this book to life. Without their tireless efforts, unwavering support, and boundless creativity, this project would not have been possible.

Firstly, we want to express our deep appreciation to the Sisa Foundation, KASO Suriname, Jungo Books, and Serendipitist Inc for making it possible for us to work on this project. We recognize that their collaboration and expertise were instrumental in creating the immersive experience we envisioned for this book. Additionally, we are indebted to Valika Smeulders (Head of the Department of History of Rijksmuseum Amsterdam) for her invaluable support in providing access to further research, which brought the historical and cultural aspects of this book to life.

We would also like to thank Sentini Grunberg for her exceptional proficiency in transforming the oral stories into this book experience, capturing the perspective we wanted to express, and for her project management skills. We also thank illustrator Francis Greenslade for creating the drawings of the main characters and surroundings with so much care and detail to our culture and historic references. We extend our sincere gratitude to Georgio Mosis for executive producing the book experience. Their professionalism and attention to detail ensured that everything ran smoothly, allowing us to concentrate on the creative process.

We cannot overstate the essential role that Andre Mosis and Laetitia Tojo played in inspiring and informing this project. As modern-day raconteurs of oral traditions, their insights and interviews were crucial to our creative process, enabling us to channel our ancestors as worthy custodians of our culture and historical heritage.

Finally, we express our heartfelt thanks to our husbands (Osasere Ogbebor and Andy van der Kamp), kids (Ma-Keyla, Sa-Yinka, Kimani and Kai), and family members for their unwavering support throughout this journey. Their unwavering belief in our vision and encouragement helped us stay focused and motivated. Our children and family were the inspiration for this work, and we hope that it will inspire them to continue to learn, grow, and pay it forward to the next generation.

As in "the Story of Sapali", we emphasize the power of collaboration and the importance of working together towards a shared goal. It is through collective efforts that we can achieve greatness, and we are honored to have had the opportunity to collaborate with such talented and dedicated individuals.

SISA2K23

Glossary

Apintie Drum

The language of the drums; also refers to a traditional percussion instrument used in many African cultures for communication, music, and in spiritual ceremonies. Apintie drums are made of wood or gourd and are played with a curved stick or hand. They are called "talking drums" because they can produce different tones and pitches that imitate the tones and inflections of human speech.

Apintieman

Apintieman is a drummer who knows the Apintie codes and rhythms and plays them on a percussion drum.

Ashanti tribe

A tribe from Ghana that was very highly regarded in her region. They were known for gold and brass craftsmanship, wood carving, furniture, and brightly colored woven cloth called *kente*.

Basiya

Slave overseers who are of African descent and used by slave masters to control and punish their own people.

Boeboe

Okanisi word for Jaguar, which is the largest New World member of the cat family. Jaguars live in the rainforest, which covers 93% of Surinam.

Bokoe

An infamous punishment utilized in the eighteenth century also referred to as the Spanish goat, freely translated from Dutch -Spaanse Bok- and executed with a firm tamarind rod.

Boobiabla

The Apintie drumming language that literally means: "the end".

Caiman

One of several species of Central and South American reptiles that are related to alligators.

Creek

A creek is a small, narrow, and often winding stream or river that flows into a larger body of water, such as a lake or a larger river.

Dutch

Language spoken by the Dutch slave traders and owners in the New World.

Fanti tribe

The Fanti tribe was a prominent West African ethnic group in 1722, engaged in trade and organized into independent states with a complex social hierarchy based on wealth and birth, and with a rich culture.

Gadoafisie

A spiritual saying, meaning God leads the way.

The Guyanas

In the 1700s, the Guyanas (also known as the Guianas) were a group of colonies in South America that were controlled by various European powers, including the Dutch, British, and French. The region included present-day Guyana, Suriname, and French Guiana. The Guyanas were primarily known for their production of sugar, rum, and other agricultural products that were cultivated on large plantations using enslaved African labor.

Igbo

The Igbo tribe was a prominent ethnic group in present-day Nigeria, with a complex society based on agriculture, trade, and social organization into independent communities. The Igbo were known for their artistic and cultural achievements, including intricate wood carvings, textiles, and musical traditions.

Kankantrie

Kankantrie is a large tree species native to Suriname. The tree belongs to the family Lecythidaceae, and its scientific name is Couroupita guianensis. The kankantrie tree is known for its large, showy flowers, which are bell-shaped and grow directly on the tree trunk and branches. The tree is culturally significant to many Indigenous and Afro-Surinamese communities, who believe that the kankantrie has spiritual and medicinal properties.

Kimonimoni

Fireflies, also known as lightning bugs, are insects that can emit light in the dark. They are known for their bioluminescence, which is the production and emission of light by living organisms. Fireflies use their light to attract mates or to warn predators of their toxicity.
In Maroon culture their presence means the absence of wild animals and presence of good spirits.

Kente

Brightly colored woven cloth from West Africa.

Lowe

It means 'to run away' in the Okanisi tribe language from Surinam.

Obiya

Obiya (also spelled Obia) is a spiritual and cultural practice that originated in West Africa and was brought to Suriname during the transatlantic slave trade. Obiya is practiced by some Afro-Surinamese and Indigenous communities in Suriname and is often used for healing, protection, and spiritual guidance. It is also associated with traditional medicine, herbalism, and divination. In Suriname, there are some negative connotations associated with Obiya due to its historical association with slavery and rebellion, and it is often viewed with suspicion and fear by mainstream society

Obiya mixture

In the story Ma-Akoeba and Sapali have made a Obiya mixture based on a combination of ground tobacco, coconut oil, and wild herbs to conceal their smell from the guard dogs of the plantation. The specific mixture they made was the Dagoe Obiya mixture. Dagoe means 'dog' in Surinamese, as this specific mixture was made to be used, so the bloodhounds on the plantation could not smell the human scent upon escape.

Panji

A long, rectangular cloth that women from the Aukan Marrin community in Surinam wrap around their waists above their navel.

Pito

A hairstyle where hair is combed to the back with a partition in the middle, with two cornrow braids on each side of the head.

Plantation

A place where slaves were held by slave owners to work on tobacco, coconut, and sugar cane.

Mandingo tribe

From the West Coast of Africa, mostly from the Mali empire, known as strong and tall people and known for their drumming and unique musical instruments.

Maroon

Maroons were communities of Africans who escaped slavery and established settlements in the Guyanas (Guyana, Suriname, and French Guyana) during the colonial era. They live in isolated areas and developed their own unique cultures, which were influenced by their African heritage and the indigenous peoples of the region. Maroon communities were often self-governed and had their own political, social, and economic systems.

Nyame Dua

Also known as the God tree in Ghana. Nyame refers to God, who is the Almighty and the Supreme Being. Dua refers to a tree, and this signifies the altar or the place of worship of God.

Okanisi tribe

One of the six Maroon tribes in Surinam. They are Aukan people.

Sand-faced people

Sapali described the people that captured her by the color of the white sand on the beach.

Slave

A person kidnapped from their homeland in Africa and brought to the New World, now known as South America.

Slave owner

Someone who has control or ownership over another human being.

Slave trader

A person who engages in the activity of capturing, transporting and selling human beings as slaves.

Made in the USA
Columbia, SC
16 October 2023

d9774290-4e88-4e57-a61f-c64b741c2a1fR01